KT-558-363

SCELIDOSAURUS

(ske-LI-doh-SAW-rus)

TYRANNOSAURUS

(tie-RAN-oh-SAW-rus)

TRICERATOPS

(try-SER-a-tops)

STEGOSAURUS

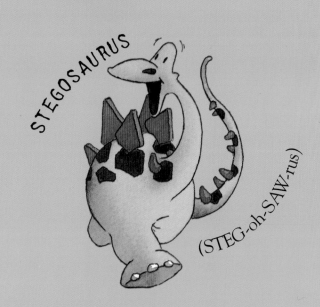

(STEG-oh-SAW-rus)

APATOSAURUS

(a-PAT-oh-SAW-rus)

ANCHISAURUS

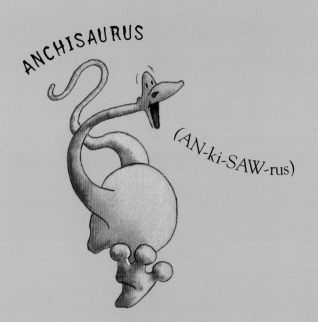

(AN-ki-SAW-rus)

SCELIDOSAURUS

(ske-LI-doh-SAW-rus)

TYRANNOSAURUS

(tie-RAN-oh-SAW-rus)

TRICERATOPS

(try-SER-a-tops)

STEGOSAURUS

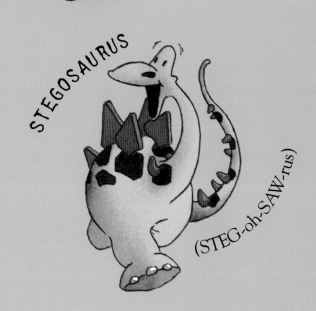

(STEG-oh-SAW-rus)

APATOSAURUS

(a-PAT-oh-SAW-rus)

ANCHISAURUS

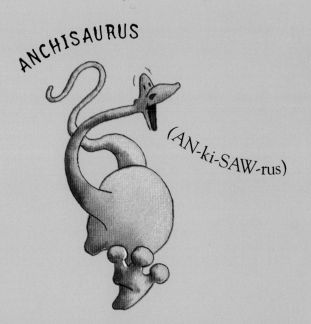

(AN-ki-SAW-rus)

For Frank Ritter who's a big Harry fan – *I.W.*

For Rhian – *A.R.*

PUFFIN BOOKS

Published by the Penguin Group

Penguin Books Ltd, 80 Strand, London WC2R 0RL, England

Penguin Group (USA), Inc., 375 Hudson Street, New York, New York 10014, USA

Penguin Books Australia Ltd, 250 Camberwell Road, Camberwell, Victoria 3124, Australia

Penguin Books Canada Ltd, 10 Alcorn Avenue, Toronto, Ontario, Canada M4V 3B2

Penguin Books India (P) Ltd, 11 Community Centre, Panchsheel Park, New Delhi – 110 017, India

Penguin Group (NZ), cnr Airborne and Rosedale Roads, Albany, Auckland 1310, New Zealand

Penguin Books (South Africa) (Pty) Ltd, 24 Sturdee Avenue, Rosebank 2196, South Africa

Penguin Books Ltd, Registered Offices: 80 Strand, London WC2R 0RL, England

www.penguin.com

First published in hardback 2003
First published in paperback 2004
7 9 10 8 6

Text copyright © Ian Whybrow, 2003
Illustrations copyright © Adrian Reynolds, 2003
All rights reserved

The moral right of the author and illustrator has been asserted

Manufactured in China

British Library Cataloguing in Publication Data
A CIP catalogue record for this book is available from the British Library

ISBN-13: 978–0–14056–952–0

Harry and the Dinosaurs make a Christmas Wish

Ian Whybrow and Adrian Reynolds

PUFFIN

It was always fun to visit Mr Oakley's farm. One time, he had some ducklings keeping warm in a box by the stove. Harry took the bucketful of dinosaurs to see.

Mr Oakley showed them one little duckling just
coming out of its shell.

Harry even held the duckling in his hands.

"Raaah! Ask him, Harry!" said the dinosaurs. "Ask Mr Oakley for a duckling to keep."

Mr Oakley said better not. They only had room for chickens over at Harry's house.

Mr Oakley let Harry and the dinosaurs ride home
in his trailer, but they were still upset.

"Shame," said Triceratops.

"Raaah!" said Tyrannosaurus. "We want a duckling!"

"Oh I *wish* we could have one!" said Harry.

It was a big wish, but it didn't work.

Maybe it was the wrong time for wishing.

At last, one cold day in the winter, the right time came.

Nan said, "Harry, will you and the dinosaurs help me stir up the Christmas pudding mixture?"

They all had a good stir and a lick – and
then they closed their eyes and they made
a *special* wish, a Christmas wish!

Harry wrote down his wish in a letter to Santa.
"What did you wish for?" asked Mum.
"A duckling!" said Harry and the dinosaurs.

"Well . . . let's look in the shops before
you send that letter," said Mum. "Just in case
you change your mind."

"Good idea!" said Nan. "I want to spend my
savings out of my egg money box!"

They all went on the bus to see the lights and the Christmas displays in the big stores.

Harry found just the right book about dinosaurs in the bookshop.

And there was plenty Harry liked in the toyshop!
So he thought of lots more things to put in his letter.

"But don't forget to say about our duckling, Harry,"
whispered the dinosaurs.

On Christmas Eve, Nan helped Harry to hang up his stocking.

"Dinosaurs don't like presents in stockings," said Harry. "They want their present in an egg."

"I see," said Nan, "then we'll leave out my money box, shall we?"

Sam said it was stupid putting out an egg.
Eggs were for Easter, not for Christmas.
That was why Harry and the dinosaurs made
RAAAH-noises all through her favourite programme.

Nan took Harry to his room to settle down.

"I've been bad to Sam, haven't I," sighed Harry. "Now I won't get my Christmas wishes."

Nan said not to get upset. Christmas wishes were special, and if you were really sorry, Santa would understand.

When Harry opened his eyes
it was Christmas morning!
  "Wake up, my Apatosaurus,
my Anchisaurus and my Triceratops!" called Harry.
  And he called, "Wake up," to his Stegosaurus
and his Scelidosaurus and his Tyrannosaurus and
all the sleepy old dinosaurs.
  They jumped up and rushed downstairs
to see what Santa had left for them.

Harry unwrapped all his presents.
"Just what I wanted!" he shouted every time.
    "What a shame," sighed the dinosaurs.
"Santa didn't bring us a duckling."
    "Wait!" said Harry. "You haven't opened your egg yet!"
    So all the dinosaurs closed their eyes, gave the egg a
warm-up and made a Christmas wish.
And guess what popped out...

...a baby pterodactyl!

"Raaah! Much better than a duckling!" said Scelidosaurus.
"Raaah! It's a flying dinosaur!" said Tyrannosaurus.
"Raaaaah to you too," said Pterodactyl.
Happy Ch-raaaaah-stmas, Harry!

SCELIDOSAURUS

(ske-LI-doh-SAW-rus)

TYRANNOSAURUS

(tie-RAN-oh-SAW-rus)

TRICERATOPS

(try-SER-a-tops)

PTERODACTYL

(TER-oh-DAC-til)

STEGOSAURUS

(STEG-oh-SAW-rus)

APATOSAURUS

(a-PAT-oh-SAW-rus)

ANCHISAURUS

(AN-ki-SAW-rus)

SCELIDOSAURUS

(ske-LI-doh-SAW-rus)

TYRANNOSAURUS

(tie-RAN-oh-SAW-rus)

TRICERATOPS

(try-SER-a-tops)

STEGOSAURUS

(STEG-oh-SAW-rus)

PTERODACTYL

(TER-oh-DAC-til)

APATOSAURUS

(a-PAT-oh-SAW-rus)

ANCHISAURUS

(AN-ki-SAW-rus)